F I R S T  S T O R Y

First Story aims to celebrate and foster creativity, literacy and talent in young people. We're cheerleaders for books, stories, reading and writing. We've seen how creative writing can build students' self-esteem and self-confidence.

We place acclaimed authors as writers-in-residence in state schools across the country. Each author leads weekly after-school workshops for up to sixteen students. We publish the students' work in anthologies and arrange public readings and book launches at which the students can read aloud to friends, families and teachers.

For more information and details of how to support First Story, see www.firststory.org.uk or contact us at info@firststory.co.uk.

It's Not That Good But...
ISBN 978-0-85748-037-8

Published by First Story Limited
www.firststory.org.uk
4 More London Riverside
London
SE1 2AU

Typesetter: Avon DataSet Ltd
Cover design: Sian Thomas
Printed in the UK by Intype Libra Ltd

It's Not That Good But...

An Anthology
BY THE FIRST STORY GROUP
AT LOXFORD SCHOOL OF SCIENCE AND TECHNOLOGY

EDITED AND INTRODUCED BY MISS STEEL AND
LAURA DOCKRILL | 2012

FIRST ▥ STORY

Fostering creativity, literacy and talent

This book is dedicated to Miss Frances Steel,
the coolest teacher in the entire universe.

Contents

Thank You

Melanie Curtis at Avon DataSet for her overwhelming support for First Story and for giving her time in typesetting this anthology.

Sian Thomas for designing the cover of this anthology and her enthusiastic support for the project.

Intype Libra for printing this anthology at a discounted rate and **Moya Birchall** and **Tony Chapman** of Intype for their advice.

Quercus Books which supported First Story in this school.

HRH the Duchess of Cornwall, Patron of First Story

The Trustees of First Story:
Beth Colocci, Charlotte Hogg, Rob Ind, Andrea Minton Beddoes, John Rendel, Alastair Ruxton, David Stephens, Sue Horner and James Wood.

The Advisory Board of First Story:
Andrew Adonis, Julian Barnes, Jamie Byng, Alex Clark, Julia Cleverdon, Andrew Cowan, Jonathan Dimbleby, Mark Haddon, Simon Jenkins, Andrew Kidd, Rona Kiley, Chris Patten, Kevin Prunty, Deborah Rogers, Zadie Smith, William Waldegrave, and Brett Wigdortz.

Thanks to:
Jane and Peter Aitken, Ed Baden-Powell, Laura Barber, The Blue Door Foundation, Josie Cameron-Ashcroft, Anthony Clake, Molly Dallas, The Danego Charitable Trust, Peter and Genevieve Davies, Martin Fiennes, the First Story Events Committee, the

First Story First Edition Club, Alex Fry, The Funding Network, Goldman Sachs Gives, Kate Harris, Kate Kunac-Tabinor, the John R. Murray Charitable Trust, Old Possum's Trust, Oxford University Press, Philip Pullman, Pitt Rivers Museum, Quercus Books, Radley College, the Sigrid Rausing Trust, Clare Reihill, The Royal Society of Literature, Chris Smith, The Staples Trust, Teach First, Betsy Tobin, Richard Tresidder, Walker Books and Hannah Westland.

Most importantly we would like to thank the students, teachers and writers who have worked so hard to make First Story a success this year.

A Word From Miss Steel...

A very short one from me as I do not want to take up space!

Just to say an enormous thank you to all the staff at Loxford, especially to Ms Turner, all of the English Department, and to Mrs Johnson for her continued support for the project and for giving us this fantastic opportunity to have a writer-in-residence.

It has been our second year of wonderful, weekly writing workshops, during which the pupils have produced astonishing pieces of work, a collection of which you are about to read. A heartfelt thank you to all who have taken part.

Finally, thank you to Laura who is the reason that we have had so many pupils staying behind after school to write; it is her inspiration that has made the writing in this anthology so outstanding and, indeed, overwhelming. Most importantly, it is because of her that we have had so much fun doing it!

A Word From Laura...

Yet another year with my glorious partner in crime 'Steely', and as we pop open another bag of *Marks and Spencer's* toffee-and-chocolate popcorn, crack the seal on our third Diet Coke, 'cheersing', we mumble and grumble and goss about the world and what we like and what we don't. As we look around us we realise for the second year in a row we have been swamped by painfully good talent, and knowing we *shouldn't* and knowing it's sort of *bad practice*, we can't help but feel a little bit too smug about how well it's all worked out. I am proud to present our incredible anthology.

Lots of love, Laura x

Tanya Ahmed

I am Tanya and I am sixteen and I was born in London. I hate the feeling when the red felt-tip runs out; when the last piece of chocolate that you've been eyeing up for the last half an hour disappears; when you can't catch the last remaining bubble floating solemnly in the air; when, in the middle of an essay, you can't help clicking back to YouTube to watch the latest craze. I have ligyrometalloacousticophobia (the fear of scraping metal noises, by the way). I love the wave of a quiff. I will always love Jacqueline Wilson's books. J'adore *Doctor Who* – I promise that one day the Daleks will take over the world. And moustaches crack me up and that's who I am.

My First Story

Tanya Ahmed

The bell,
The rush,
The turquoise door,
The eager wait,
The distant smiles,
The hugs,
The kisses,
The bold pink lippy,
The chairs and tables,
The bags,
The pens and papers,
The discussion,
The gossip,
The jokes,
The nibbles,
The chocolates,
The wrappers,
The theme,
The writing,
The scribbles and doodles,
The biting of the pen lids,
The reading:
It's not that good but...

A Day In The Life Of My Feet

Tanya Ahmed

So, in the morning,
I dive into a pink fluffy rug,
I feel the coldness of the bathroom tiles,
The wetness of the water from the shower,
The soapiness from the bubbles,
The roughness from the dry towel,
The silky, coolness of the cream,
The warm softness of the socks which clothe me,
The pinch, as my master adjusts my socks,
The security, as the shoe protects my sole,
The soreness from the constant walking in school,
The painful strain as I run in the gym,
The cold, dirty, hardness of the concrete garden floor,
The fresh exposure of the removal of my sock,
The sticky wetness as I step on a piece of chewing gum,
The soft, bouncy padding of my flip flops,
The warmth as I rest, covered by the blanket in my bed.

My Red Stool

Tanya Ahmed

My mother was a gardener who used to plant all sorts of wondrous flowers ranging from daisies to daffodils to roses and bluebells. I used to watch in awe as I sat on my bold red stool admiring her flawless skill of coating the flowers in a rich, silky hazelnut soil; she caressed them and patted them in their place. Only she could perform this magnificent craft. Once or twice I attempted it myself, to mimic her effortless talent, but failed incredibly. I remember the smell of this brown dirt, a very strong smell, a sort of musty, dying smell; a smell hard for one to describe. I remember the smell of the Flash window cleaner my mother used often to clean the greenhouse. Consequently, the sun's rays bounced dancingly, creating a spectacular rainbow effect, an unforgettable performance.

And here I stand now.

Dark moss and green vines are infecting the greenhouse. Brown mud stains are splashed across the glass, leaving a dirty residue behind. The tint of the window resembles the colour of stained coffee. Transparent, patterned cobwebs scrawl across the corners of the windows. Creamy, grey and dull orange stones are mixed into the soil, which is now dried up and shriveled into clumpy colonies. The hazelnut colour has vaporised like a watery

IT'S NOT THAT GOOD BUT...

brown being mixed in with too much white; a sense of paleness and ghoulishness represent the colours of the soil now. Overgrown weeds contaminate the rest of the garden, some of which are almost to my waist. As I turn slightly to my right, I notice something lost and abandoned in the corner, like a lost puppy or teddy. Suddenly a flush of warmth hugs me as I feel a past connection. A paleish pink patchy stool covered in mud leans against the brick wall. My stool. The rain eroded the memories and the sun absorbed the life of it.

364 Days Of Waiting

Tanya Ahmed

The crispy white flake landed gracefully amongst its fellow peers as the sound of bells became more dominant. I stared outside my window with my nose pressed against the glass. I smelt the golden turkey, hibernating in my mother's oven, waiting to be cut open and distributed among my family. The humongous Christmas tree stood proud as the sparkling balls decorated its vibrant green leaves. The 364 days of waiting.

Nashrath Yasmin

I am my music. I am my books. I am my drawings. I am my food.
I am my friends. I am my family. I am Nashrath. I am Yasmin.

Delirious

Nashrath Yasmin

I lost my mind.
I can't seem to find it.
Will you help me?

Kemal Cakli

My name is Kemal, I am sixteen years old. I love to read, write, act and joke. I can see myself being a future world leader and legend... maybe.

Want to know more? Read all about it, *it's not that good... but...*

They Are Our Future

Kemal Cakli

-Welcome -

Click-clack-clack-click.

The virtual words, sentences, messages are being written as we speak, if you want to call it *written*.

Everywhere you go, you will hear it; you will hear them. You will hear the way they are used: to write letters; to complete work; to write sick ransoms that will one day be seen by a parent desperately wanting their child back.

They are beginning to control the world, controlling the latest generation, who will one day be 'our future'.

They have already used themselves to create abbreviations for words that legends have created and used.

Click-clack-click-clack.

They are keys, like footsteps, following your every move. They are following your every thought, *creating* your every thought. Making their own music, music that transforms one into a different world, an alternate universe.

You're using them right now.

Their ignorant and obsessive sounds lure you in, you begin to enjoy it.

Quills died out, then came the pencil.
Pencils began to snap, then came the pen.
Pens began to break, then came them.
They cannot die out, they cannot snap and they cannot break.
They are immortal, long-lasting, they are forever.
They are mere letters on the opposite side of a screen.
They are our future.

Click-clack-click-clack.

-Shut down-

This Body Will Be No More

Kemal Cakli

There he goes again,
Showing me off.
How many more steroids
Is he going to scoff?

He's inked my look
He's stained my skin,
Every competition,
He has to win!

I give him hair
He cuts it away
Bald on the sides
And some strands to stay?

He barely wears a thing,
Leaves my bones to shiver.
The diet hurts my stomach
And the drink kills my liver.

But one day he'll do too much
And make my muscles too sore,
My heart will burst, my brain will freeze
This body will be no more.

Changed For Good

Kemal Cakli

Heart beating?... *Check*!
Lungs breathing?... *Check*!
Blood flowing?... *Oh No*!

There's a cut! There's a cut!

Cells? *Where are you*? See to this cut... immediately!

Go on... keep working, there are no breaks when you have to work for this big fella. Think of me! I have all you guys to look after, to make sure you're doing your job, but also I get hurt when 'the boss' gets into a fight. I get wet when he decides he wants to go for a dip in the pond! *Yeah*... I may look hard, rough, jagged and scaly on the outside, but inside, I'm just a layer of blubber... *Literally*!

Guys... guys? *Why have you stopped*?
Heart beating?... *Oh No*!
Heart breathing?... *Where's the oxygen*?
Blood flowing?... *It's seeping out of me*!

I've never felt that kind of blade before!

I like working for my new boss. All I do is get carried around now, I don't even need to tell *lipstick*, *keys* or even *phone* what to do! I just wait until the almighty 'hand' reaches in and grabs whatever it wants. All I have to do is show myself off, and now I don't even need to move. I've got an opening up there, so even my inside gets to see the light!

Ahh, this is the perfect job.
Lipstick closed?... *Check!*
Keys clinging?... *Check!*
Phone ringing?... *Check.*

The Mirror Speaks To Me

Kemal Cakli

It screams out.
Pink, red, brown, soft, smooth.
It tells me that I have two red rivers and speech,
A mouth that opens when I have a thought and closes when I
　　shut down.
That just above, the skin waits for the strands of daggers to pierce
　　through it eventually, causing me to cut it off again.
It whispers that the air rushes and flows, through the two gaps of

nothing that will one day turn to a soft stream of oxygen.
One that will, eventually, stop inhaling forever.
It yells as the craters and creases of my being will lead to my two
spheres of sight.

The Most Amazing Person In The World

Kemal Cakli

Hi, I'm the most amazing person in the world. The one who makes you laugh, cry, happy, sad and so on... *Who am I?* You might ask, you tell me... It's hard isn't it? I could be your mum, your dog, even your smiley English teacher who blushes every time someone comes into the room. I could even be *you*. Think about it, you could easily be the most amazing person in the world, because only you know what you've been through, what you've done.

What you're going to do.

Raqayya Arshad

My passion is writing. I am described in many ways but personally I would say I am quite tall with curly dark hair and your everyday teen. But when I write, my stories overtake reality and the boundaries between fiction and reality blur. And that's the best thing: being able to let your imagination control you.

An Open Door...

Raqayya Arshad

I press against her weathered lean body and grasp her outstretched golden hand, begging for comfort from the harsh outside world. I lean against her wearily for support, waiting for her frail body to bow in relief from the heavy strain of the brass hinges that clasp onto her thin torso. I listen out for the hushed sigh that escapes her and resonates against the claustrophobic walls that lean in on me. Suffocating. I breathe in the heavy scent of old wood. She opens up her arms in a loving embrace; it is filled with chairs and a soft bed that whispers to me, enticing me with its satin sheets. I sag against her. Home.

Python

Raqayya Arshad

Sirens of alarm, dark nightmares unfold.

Numb.
My enemy closes in on me.
This foreign pulse invading my powerless body,
Crumbling into oblivion under its compelling strength.

Desperate.
My poisoned body collapses beneath me as he whispers those
    words of doom.

Venomous.
My toxic snake slithers inside me.
Seeking revenge in this raging war,
Lashing out against my weak veins.
Annihilation.

Defeat.
Shattered by my own reflection. Lost in this draining battle.
I live in my former shadow as I slowly deteriorate.
Glancing down memory lane at the past me,
The beautiful me.

What have I become?
An outcast...
I am running out of time.

Kind strangers.
Unknown, unnamed; poking me, prodding me... and rescuing
me?

Reborn.
Thankful for a second chance
The lethal venom dripping away
As I breathe in the fresh smell of new life.
I am the survivor, I have won the jackpot.
At last, free from this prison. Free from this cell of cancer.

Benish Sheikh

My name's Benish and I'm a fourteen-year-old girl; my birthday's on May 1st. I live in Ilford in the Borough of Redbridge which is in the UK. I've always had a deep love for writing and stories because you can use words in all sorts of ways and for showing different perspectives. A lot of things inspire my writing but there are three main things: music, art and literature; because with them you can interpret the different aspects of something in new ways. That's probably why I've always loved anime shows since I was little because they incorporate all three of those to create an interesting story. My writing is also inspired by basic aspects of everyday life because I like to see things in every possible way and in more detail. I then use music, literature and people's perspectives to inspire me to write about those things in an interesting and hopefully positive way. I aspire to be a writer in the future and hope that I inspire others with my writing.

Change In Forecast

Benish Sheikh

The weather is a recurring change. Every single day I look up into the sky countless times and, if the sun is shining or the dark blanket of the sky is hugging the stars, I watch and admire it. Or if the clouds are hiding the sun away I don't look too long and turn away because I know what's coming: rain.

The weather: isn't that what you talk about in the awkward situations?

Well this does have meaning because the weather's recurring change each day is just like your change. One day you're smiling and holding your arms wide open like the sun's rays and then the next you're raining down on me with your cold words and I shiver to the cold, feeling drowned. You're so unpredictable and unreliable, just like the weather. Even if you had a broadcast of your emotions you'd still never know what was coming next: be told the sun would be out one day, its rays dancing on the pavements, and then the thunderstorm rages in the sky.

Remember when you got sunburnt? Even the sun's angry at you. Stay friends with you? You're kidding. We were never friends in the first place.

Pretty Perspective

Benish Sheikh

The soft duvet of black and brown falls gently, framing my cream-coloured canvas of a complexion. The dark chocolate-coated pupils centre the white marbles. The soft duvet of black and brown falls gently, framing the cream-coloured canvas of a complexion. The pitch-black irises dance and glimmer surrounded by the dark chocolate-coated pupils centring the white marbles. The fans of eyelashes cluster around the spiralling marbles.

Under the spiralling marbles rest pink tulips which flutter apart in full bloom. As the pink tulips part, the fans of eyelashes emerge gently up and down making the spiralling marbles dazzle in the flickering light.

As the tulips part they utter the words, 'They say looks don't matter but what does that really mean?' What they mean by this is that your appearance shouldn't affect you in any way as looks are not important, which is true. But in a sense they do matter, as they are how your loved ones remember you. They remember the beauty in you that you didn't always see yourself.

Everyone can be and is beautiful in their own way.

You're beautiful in the eyes of others so see yourself as beautiful too. Take a good look at yourself and think kind thoughts and you'll realise how beautiful you really, truly are, inside and out. All you need to do is use a prettier perspective.

Naadiyah Mohammad

Hello, my name is Naadiyah. I'd like to take this moment to say that in all honesty there's no point in talking to me while I'm reading because I'm not going to listen to you. If you feel any pain from these words, then laugh. It helps.

Who You Are

Naadiyah Mohammad

Who are you?
Are you the anguish that squeezes your heart?
The fire you sometimes see flaring in your eyes?
Or maybe the sugar-coated words that slip from your lips,
Sometimes turned into a treacherous web of silken lies?

Are you a drop of water in the ocean?
A sparkling crystal, alone at times,
Falling freely, freely, freely...
Until you're surrounded all at once?

Who are you?
Are you the words that you write,
Drawn from the depth of a moonless night,

Put together hastily under flickering candlelight?
Inky words that ebb and flow with emotion,
Your very sweat and blood,
Poured into a new skin?

You are who you choose to be.
A different day, a different person.

A different dream, every new season.

But the most important thing by far
Is to let nobody, by what they do or say,
Change what makes you who you are.

Mohamed Mardadi

My name is Mohamed, I am seventeen and I live in Ilford but was born in East Africa. I am influenced by my surroundings and different things going on around me; things that affect me or affect others. I like giving my insight and perspective on issues that others may fear to talk about or don't feel comfortable talking about. My work is intended for performance and I use that to give my work another breath of life.

Imagine

Mohamed Mardadi

Imagine every human was all the same colour,
Imagine she was your sister and he was your brother.
Imagine a world with no wars and just peace,
Imagine a world with no problems and just ease.
Imagine a world where poverty was unknown,
Imagine everybody had a place to call home.
Imagine a life with diversity and unity,
Imagine this world to be one big community.
Imagine happiness, smiles and no tears,
Imagine togetherness, love and no fears.
Imagine there being no pain and no struggling,
Imagine there being no such thing as suffering.
Imagine the world with so much of a difference,
Imagine everyone was known for their existence.
Imagine no one felt lost in this world as a victim,
Imagine going back to the old days, because I miss them.
Imagine living your life as a kid, just innocent,
Imagine not going through life-changing incidents.
Imagine your only problem was choosing what food to eat,
Imagine we didn't have to watch our close ones just fall asleep.
Imagine getting rid of all of our dark days,
Imagine nobody in the world felt a heartache.

Imagine no dying so we didn't have to part ways,
Imagine knowing that tomorrow is a bright day.
Imagine waking up feeling happier than ever,
Imagine that you lost all your stresses and your pressure.
Imagine you didn't have to smile to cover up your pain,
Imagine nobody had any hate on your name.
Imagine that all your dreams just happened to come true,
Imagine having no dilemmas and obstacles to jump through.
Imagine feeling happy for the person that you are,
Imagine making a name for yourself and getting far.
Imagine pursuing your ambitions and then achieving,
Imagine all the joy that you will be receiving.
Imagine standing up for what you believe in,
Imagine success without failure intervening.

Imagination can take you places that you've never been,
Imagination can take you places that you've never seen.
Imagination can be a catalyst to make reality from all your dreams,
Imagination can pull you closer no matter how far it seems.
Imagination is the freedom of thought which lies inside,
So take imagination with you through your journey in life –
Imagine.

Smile

Mohamed Mardadi

A smile is able to cover up pain,
Cure a problem – make a change,
A smile can hide your fears.

A smile could hold truths and lies,
Tell a story through its wide – stretch,
A smile can show you care.

A smile can brighten up a person's day,
Help them take their worries away –
A smile can wipe your tears.

A smile can speak a thousand words,
As melodious as the singing of birds,
A smile can bring you near.

A smile can be the drive you need,
When you're feeling low – can't succeed,
A smile will make things clear.

A smile is like the touch of a mother,
Love and warmth like no other,

A smile is the silence you hear.

A smile can be the icon of life,
Diverse in its uses – a shining light,
A smile is the beauty we share.

A smile can rid your hurt.
Make clean of what is dirt,
A smile so sweet, so dear.

A smile asks why you are crying.
Keeps you going, keep trying,
A smile is the enemy of fear.

A smile is giving and receiving,
Tells the world how you're feeling,
A smile is happiness.

Changes

Mohamed Mardadi

As a kid I was innocent, filled up with laughter,
I used to live for the moment, never worry about what's after.
I never thought that my life could change as it did,

Now I'm wishing I was small again to live life as a kid.
My only problems before were choosing what cereal to eat in the
    morning,
Or how to get out of trouble when Mum gave me a lot of
    warnings.
But now it seems like everything around me has got changes,
The same friends I used to play cops and robbers with are now
    strangers.
It's funny because when I was young I had dreams too,
But I didn't believe any of them would be true.
I used to listen to rap music without understanding the words,
But I was still able to rap word for word in every verse.
Back then English for me was all just gibberish,
But now I can speak my mind in this language like I always
    wished.
I had all my thoughts squashed in and trapped inside,
But this is something I thank God for – this sense of pride,
Believe me this is something quite hard to understand,
The process of learning and the transition from a boy to man.
Not once did I understand the power of expressing,
The beauty of words, its influences and its blessings.
As you grow older you seem to think quite deep,
Like why do we cry when we're born – what's the reason for
    sleep?
I see as I grow some things excite me, other things they hurt me,
But I guess that's just the effect of this beautiful journey.
That's life I guess.

Ashir Nadeem

Hi, I'm Ashir.

I'm twelve years old. I'm about 5 foot 9 with hair that's all over the place, frustratingly messy eyebrows, strong glasses and big, scarred hands. I'm sort of a hybrid between a nerd and an... anti-nerd. I have a reasonably deep voice but I don't think it suits me. I have huge feet. I like spamming and trolling and writing, online games and swimming and boxing and fighting and eating and war films and generally any films and writing stories and reading both fiction and non-fiction and ice cream and pizza and fruit and certain vegetables and cake and telling cheesy jokes and *Angry Birds* and history. I hate those brats on *Sweet 16*, stepping on Lego pieces, racism and all sorts of discrimination, bullying, aubergines, brussel sprouts and gangster wannabies. I'm into hard rock and metal (music, of course), and I have a fanatical hatred of rap.

I want to be an author, history teacher, philosopher, psychiatrist and an IT manager but I'll settle for two. I have no inspirations aside from my parents for giving me more opportunities to explore anything at any time than I think most will get in their lifetime.

I am a very faithful agnostic. I'm stubborn, arrogant and adamant. I'm extremely philosophical and think about things very deeply. I express some of my beliefs through my writing, which is why it has become such a huge aspect in my life. I like ice cream.

P.S I'm thirteen now, and getting a Kindle for my birthday. Too lazy to scroll to the top of the page to edit it. Oh yeah, I'm very lazy. Should have put that in at the top but I sort of forgot. Oh yeah, I'm very forgetful. The irony is I have trouble writing short stories, as I'm accustomed to writing huge essays and stuff. I have one at home that I'm hoping to get published once I've finished it, but that won't be for a long time. I'll stop talking now.

The Vista

Ashir Nadeem

The purple of dawn benignly rested in the morning sky, its fibres entangled in the orange of morning. The planes of hills ran far out, marking the horizon with the swerving tops of the natural mounds. The blindingly luminous sun seemed to sit idly between a smooth curve on the bumpy vista, warming the atmosphere with its burning, apocalyptic light. The few clouds that dominated the vibrant heavens slothfully moved towards the end of the awe-invoking panorama that sat before Baron.

He shifted uncomfortably on the rocky cliff that supported his light bulk, allowing his hardy eyes to rest their sight upon the steppes that shimmered and glowed under the thin coats of fresh rain a thousand feet below him. He cherished the warming safety of a perfect asylum: a sanctuary of peace far deeper than he could ever experience on the fields of blood and death he was accustomed to killing over. A place of meditation and contemplation. A place of thought. Such serenity did the place offer; the strong aroma of rain continued to spit over him gently; the cold, relieving bursts of wind expelled the comfortable warmth of the sluggish sun and wafted the fine grass blades that trembled on the earth's surface like the emerald fur of a peaceful beast folk. Such amity, such harmony, it reminded Baron of the time he spent as a child in the flowerful gardens of Macedonia. Little did he know at the time that in the future he would be so grateful, even for being whipped, smacked, punched and pushed against the cynical Persians with the ruthless tyrant, Alexander the Great, to lead them across the entire world.

Such beauty reminded him of his wife and two sons. The thought instantly filled him with the longing and homesickness that dwindled his morale the more he concentrated on it. Thus, he dismissed the thought with no regard for anything that pleased him and continued exploring the glorious landscape with his vigorous, ever-bounding sight.

He grimaced as he stretched his arms out wearily. Then he dropped his hands to the rock heavily and turned his head to scan the skies over his shoulder. It had lost its luminous, vivid colours and had died into a blue that darkened as it stretched to either of the boundaries of his vision. It was nearing twilight, and he had been sitting exactly where he sat now for three hours; the vista never ceased to interest and relax him.

Wearily, he lifted his feet from their position hanging off the edge of the cliff, shifted back with his arms and, supporting his weight with his four scarred limbs, he rose to stand imperiously, looking over the world waiting idly for him to stab the Macedonian flag into its fruitful soil. He turned with a rough motion and gaited towards low ground.

Within twenty minutes, wherein he had alternated between sprinting and jogging over the cliff that rested with the skies, he had stumbled upon the opposite edge of the precipice that would lead back to camp. It wasn't such a steep climb down, but nonetheless it was dangerous and rough, so he made his way hesitantly, hooking his hands onto whatever the crag offered to them, often making precipitous jumps that significantly cut the time to reach the forest. The air was noticeably becoming thicker as he climbed down the cold, coarse surface.

Finally, he made the last leap onto the mud that his footwear sank into. He shook the dirt off vigorously as he hobbled to a boiling summer spring, the water cascading down into a small, steaming pool, limping as he had bloodied his right leg a bit on the way down.

He took five steps, and a feathered arrow abruptly whizzed a few inches past him, a trail of thin wind slapping Baron's face.

He had left his armour and weaponry at his marquee, but a gold-encrusted sheath concealing the blade of a long serrated dagger embellished his back, the plain rubber pommel protruding between his neck and right shoulder blade. Hastily, he unsheathed it, revealing its chilling, thirsty scimitar blade, adjusted his fingers to slip into the curves forged off the pommel, and transformed his casual stance into the posture of a Macedonian warrior, his long hair agitating his neck. The blade guarding his complete torso, he proceeded to scan the dense forestation that surrounded him, the ancient trees jeering at him, for any slight motion. He was met with disappointment – none of his five senses could seek out a trace of anything. The scent of rain wafted into his nostrils; crickets and the bubbling of water dug into his ears and his eyes observed only the indifferent, idle trees which stood proud and strong against the occasional battering the wind could potentially offer. But he wasn't convinced. Slowly and tentatively, he shifted towards where the arrow base protruded from the rocky face that guarded his back and squinted suspiciously at the smooth wood, his facial muscles tensing as he tried to decipher its origin. The rich feathers that blanketed its base were undoubtedly Persian, he thought, employing his experience of the fierce people to walk him to a result. Reassured, he approached the forest, entering its undiscovered depths.

The crooked trees cast an ominous shadow upon the earth that dawned on Baron like a beast patiently waiting for the right time to leap on its prey. He moved through the no man's land in a cautious, crouched gait, his short sword at the ready.

Without warning, a sharp movement caught the peripheral of his eyes.

Instantly and instinctively, he snapped his head right with a rapid motion and locked his eyes onto his to-be victim before he advanced out of his vision, watching as he sprinted around seemingly with no objective in mind.

A vicious, wild scream erupted behind him, followed by two others of differing tone and volume.

He turned and before him were four warriors clothed in plain loincloths and head-robes dirtied with debris. In their right hands settled cutthroat knives of varying lengths and shapes but used in the same style; and rough wooden shields, painted with a single, elaborate eye, rested in the grip of their left.

They charged towards him, but he stood his ground, moving not an inch.

The first soldier attempted a daring jump to overwhelm Baron, but he found a small flaw in the taut defence the shield offered and exploited it immediately, thrusting the blade into the soldier's soft flesh; a rivulet of maroon blood poured down from the protrusion; the soldier's deafening cry shook the quiet jungle.

Another soldier was approaching quickly. He unsheathed the grimy blade from the lungs of his first kill and braced himself for impact, his brawny left arm shielding his torso as his dagger hung patiently in the temperate air.

The second fighter approached him using a different tactic: ducking down and covering himself with his shield as he hacked his feet.

He jumped over the saw hastily and landed with a smash of his leg onto his foe's shield, breaking a Persian arm and denting the wood with the brute strength of the stomp. He used the same leg to smash the shield out of the combatant's grip and slit his neck with a smooth, lightning slash, the scarlet blood squirting out from the wound as the victim wordlessly raised his hand to his neck before tumbling to the floor messily with a startled gape.

He kicked the corpse far enough to retrieve the land, which two Persians had the idiotic idea of stepping foot onto, and jiffies later came a frenzy of intense sword fighting. Baron grimaced as he struggled to fend off the two wild fighters, confronted by the skill of agility which their brethren had not performed.

Out of nowhere, a second arrow sped towards him from a distant tree, aimed so inaccurately it was heading towards one of the couple of soldiers he was engaged in vigorous combat with. Thus, whilst making sure not to be pushed back himself, he did not make an attempt to press on to the soldiers until the arrow sharply stabbed through the left-most Persian's back, followed by a steady stream of red pouring out of his groaning mouth, cascading down onto his clothes. The death dropped the intensity of the battle and, with one more to finish, he pushed the lifeless body aside, stealing his space, and hacked the edge of his dagger into the last fighter's hip before he could do so much as twitch his arm. He withdrew its serrated blade out of the cleaved flesh and let gravity take the cadaver down as a third arrow was shot from the distance, but with weak power, enabling him to catch it with a swift reach and to throw it indifferently onto the soil as he sped towards where the arrows were originating from. A small brook of sweat was beginning to accumulate around his forehead.

As soon as he had taken a few steps, the archer revealed himself to be mounted as he galloped around Baron, a favoured tactic, he observed. He shot yet another arrow as he circled around him, only to be sharply deflected by the rough pommel of his dagger. Soon after, he charged out from hiding the very warrior who had begun the ambush, now equipped with a huge eight-foot spear and a wooden shield. The mounted Persian released yet another missile at him, tearing apart the solid air in its way. Seeing a chance, the footed warrior contributed his spear to the assault, hurling the javelin at Baron with impressive elegance. But he simply ducked to the ground, allowing the projectiles to soar over him with an insolent smile. A surge of energy channeled into him from the air, feeling unstoppable, inescapable, inexorable...

He got back up on his feet and tracked both opponents with his piercing eyes, remaining in the same stance in the same position. Realising that if they both co-ordinated an assault it would kill him, however, he abruptly changed course and charged at the horseman before he could move out of range. He leaped himself up into the air, transforming his bulk into a tight ball as he soared in the air. Just before he hit the soldier, he sprung his legs forward and butted the man off the horse, causing him to be blown metres into the distance as Baron landed chaotically onto the mud. On the other side of the clearing, the now-unequipped combatant searched the field for a weapon, buying Baron some time to run up to the pummeled opponent and wrestle his dagger down to his throat, beheading him with a relentless hack before turning back to the foot warrior, the dry blood on his dagger's blade rehydrated. His final opponent scowled with frustration and braced himself for death as Baron strode confidently towards him.

Baron, however, knowing the large sword that his foe had scavenged from one of his felled brothers, sheathed his dagger, retreated to the freshest carcass and stole the bow, hanging the quiver around his back.

Outraged, the beast ran towards him with an ever-reverberating cry. Just then, Baron decided to see how his rival would cope with his own tactic against him. In fact, he was so bold he decided to improve the strategy. He locked his bow and started jogging around his opponent, gaining speed as he went, careful not to trip over the scattered bodies or weapons that covered the small glade. Then, as the wild man sped after him, he leaped on to a tree and ran on its surface before gravity had a chance to bring him down. Stabled by hooking his arm around a thick bush, its leaves buckling as it supported his entire weight, he used the hand of the hooked arm to relieve his left arm of holding both the composite bow and the locked arrow at its tip, and he retrieved the missile and hastily released it at the Persian. He was, however, untrained in the art of archery, and thus the arrow clumsily dropped a couple of metres away from his target. Frustrated, he made a daring bound to the furthest yet reachable tree and landed elegantly on the curve between the trunk and a thick branch. He locked another projectile and released the taut string. Unexpectedly it flew towards the soldier, who stupidly used his hand to defend his face instead of simply manoeuvring the missile, which, in his case, was quite an opportunity. The thin arrow pierced his skin and tore straight through his hand, an echoing groan following, but he belligerently picked it out in spite of the pain it would cause, grimacing and shouting behind grinding teeth. As soon as the metal was torn from his bleeding flesh, he threw it aside gently with a moan of relief, and adjusted the grip on the two-handed sword he impressively managed to keep hold of with his weaker arm.

Feeling no need to move trees, having successfully hindered his opponent, he discharged another arrow, and having limited time to react, his foe raised a brown shoulder-pouch, astounding Baron that he had renewed his stupidity when he could have simply shifted out of the way. The iron arrowhead slammed into the coarse leather, piercing it, and went so deep that it penetrated the hidden end. Astonishingly, dozens of tiny diamonds, gold orbs and precious stones cascaded to the damp soil, some pushed out with such a force that they hit their owner in the face, and one of the smallest diamonds stabbed into his eye, maiming him as he hurled to the floor heavily. Seeing a palpable chance to exploit, Baron's burning heart pounded with excitement as he locked an arrow, aimed, and shot it straight below his neck.

It hit its target.

He leaped to the ground, submitting to gravity's grasp, painfully landing on his injured leg with a scowl, proceeding to approach the Persian's struggling body with an imperious atmosphere, the ends of his lips faintly curved into a bold smile. His heart smashed against his bruised chest and scared back excruciatingly; a rivulet of thin sweat was flowing down from his long, damp hair, as he limped to his last kill, either putting him out of his misery or simply increasing it with a powerful heel-kick that broke his straight spine with a click. Almost immediately, with no regard for his idle surroundings, he began to collect the diamonds from the forest floor, and then opened his full hand above a small belt-pouch of his own, the stones tumbling down and landing softly and inaudibly into the pocket. He advanced a few steps and bent down sluggishly to retrieve the miniscule shoulder bag that lay beside the rotting remains, stretching his limbs simultaneously. He rose harmoniously, his heart mollified, and stretched the opening with his thumb and index finger, ignoring the few stones that fell to the earth from the two neat piercings. They shone in the deadening sunlight even more as he elongated the aperture of the pouch and continued to pour its contents into the plain, slightly smaller pocket of his own. But as the metals and stones plummeted down, an ancient-looking, beige paper came with them. Intrigued, he obtained it from the storage and closed the flap. Tattooed onto the paper were words written in the finest calligraphy, definitely of royal standard. He quickly scanned through the letter, instinctively deeming it of little importance to him, seeing as it belonged to the Persian, but nonetheless looked for anything that could reveal a hint about plans of Persian resistance.

Then, fearing his eyes had tricked him, he reread the whole letter, this time with the utmost solemnity.

He read it again.

Dread emanated in his gut, bemusement accumulated in his mind and fear ignited his heart. It was not only physical now, but also psychological warfare he was to engage in with the Persians. Extreme worry infected his conscience and spread like a tumour, refueling his pounding heart.

He sprinted towards camp with all of the remaining vitality he could muster, running so fast you would have immense difficulty tracking him. His hair flew in the wind that reflected around him, carrying it more firmly than a hand could.

Signs of gold bring you Macedonians to its source like sheep would a fresh farm of grass! You people are a skilled folk in the art of the warrior, an art that we clearly lack; but we do have an advantage, and that is merely intelligence.

Hopefully when you revisit your camp you will learn not to abandon the people who rely on your commandeering purely for the comfort of a harmonious panorama, and hopefully King Alexander will demote a general that is so diminutive a challenge to me that it is indeed quite insulting.

Signed,
King Darius of Persia

Rim Karama

'I am Buzz Lightyear. I come in peace...'

... Nope, it's just Rim Karama. I'm sixteen years old, I'm Muslim and I live with my Mum, Dad, three sisters and two brothers. I'm quite a chilled-out person and love a good ol' laugh. Annoy me and I'll annoy you back. It's fun. I don't like sarcasm, unless it's either: 1) used by me, or 2) hilarious [in which case, I'll let it slide]. I come from a football-loving family. By this I mean hardcore cheering and full-on competitiveness. I have a 'nothing' accent. I prefer blue ink pens to any other colour. I love badges, key rings and feathers. Phineas or Firb? It's gotta be Firb! The awkward moment after you've done your exams, had a convo with a clever friend and realise that your answers were different, yeah? Well I'm in that situation a lot. I love my funky, multicoloured socks. I have yet to figure out my own signature. It changes daily. I love art; drawing when I'm bored entertains me; movies/films, old or new, bring me in, I just can't get enough of them (Massive vibes for the big screens!); headphones in (full volume) on a long journey home from somewhere; genius creations (try it sometime). I talk a lot, sometimes too much. I laugh a lot, again, sometimes too much. Anime and manga-style drawing controls the pencil I hold. I don't read that much, but when I get hold of a book, I'm gone. I laugh at my own jokes when I feel it's necessary. We all do it. Don't lie. I want to go around the world someday. I want to do something creative in the future, write, draw, blah... something I enjoy and gets me loads of money, not sure. Anyways, that's the end, my friends. Peace outttt.

Oh, by the way, I'm a girl. I'm sure you've realised, but if not, re-read what I just wrote. Sometimes it helps?

Design

Rim Karama

Design your imagination.
Using it requires no hesitation.
It's one's creations, a sensation, a personal fascination.
Take advantage of it.
It will take you to places that only you can create.
It's a part of you, a trait.
Never disturb when it's in action, wait.
You design a world, a character, a vision.
It requires precision.
On a pedestal: a high position.
Don't let it drive you, let it be driven.
No need to ask for permission.
Use it whenever you feel necessary.
It changes depending on the person,
Yet it remains ordinary.
Something owned by everybody.
But it's you that makes it extraordinary;
Your own story, expose the inner glory.
It's the mind that it possesses.
Keep it a secret; dare to guess it.
It releases all your stresses.
Reveal your creative side!

Unwrap the essential prize!
And then you find that there's a gift inside,
A companion that helps you write…
…draw, think.
You notice there's a link.
A source that beats knowledge, but lets your mind sink –
Sink into an undiscovered path. Take it. Resist the urge to blink.
It's a painting, something that you're creating,
A human's making.
Can you feel your outer shell breaking?
The colour and joy of your insides inflating.
Design it. Design it how you desire. Design it and let it inspire.
Leave time to admire.
Design it and be familiar with your creation, the amazement.
Design the one thing you can: your imagination.

Dream Big

Rim Karama

Nothing will ever get bigger than a person's dream, so *dream big*.
Let it take over your mind, see what you can find.
They say when you dream, you're often blind:
Blind from reality, but make your dreams a reality.
Prove them wrong. You may be sleeping or just thinking, but you
    were living it all along.
Dream big.
Bigger than you feel your mind can handle,
You search for what you want to do,
Who you want to see, let it be, let it find you.
You want to be doctor, a musician or a dancer -
Don't give in, you'll find the answer.
Dream bigger than you did last year,
Let it be a resolution, let it be your own creation.
But the key is patience, it will come, just believe it.
Let it collide with your thoughts: feel it.
Make your family proud, for you were able to achieve it.
You dug deep, and even though it faded, you made it.
Take it with both hands and contain it.
Dream big.
Don't think about who you are offending,
Think about the message you are sending,

About the younger generation taking the path that you are
     lending:
Passion. Can you sense it? It's time to stop pretending.
It's like a pencil to a paper: words, art, something you can add
     onto later.
You want to be an athlete, a teacher, an actor or a journalist.
Never resist.
Take a shot, never miss.
Make a list, a letter to yourself, a promise, I insist.
Make people wonder and ask what it means, for it's never what it
     seems,
Let the light beam,
Let it take you to a different world,
A world that, to many, is unseen,
Let it gleam, for nothing will ever get bigger than a person's
     dream,
So *dream big.*

Tangle Me. I Dare You.

Rim Karama

I'm Laura Lace. I tangle myself and deliberately loosen my arms, my dusty concrete arms that sharply hit the ground whenever she walks at a pace that's faster than usual. But don't worry, there's a glowing white underneath it all, under the *filth*. And that's the truth. Take it how you please. Though my actions always have consequences, I never fail to take a risk, do what many others would see as deadly, jeopardising my place in her collection. But it's only a bit of harmless fun, payback even. I know I'm needed here, we all are, I'm just seen as less important.

She stumbles, she falls… oh well. She'll get used to it. She deserves it. She pulls me a lot and creates an unwanted knot in my stomach. It hurts. She has me strapped onto one of her old trainers – the worn-out kind, useful when needed but not appealing to the eye. I see millions of me, when I'm left alone on the shoe rack or scatted across the corridor: copies and copies. But they're colourful and bright; they're new and are placed on expensive, designer shoes, unlike myself for instance. I sometimes get jealous, but I'm good when it comes to containing myself. Believe it or not, that used to be me. The one everyone looks at, drooling over, you know, the one everyone aspires to be some day. But yeah, *that* shortly ended.

She only wears me when she's walking her dog, playing footy at the park, and 'running to the shops for a sec'. Those seem to be part of her daily routine most of the time. I hate it when she runs; I get all dizzy and forget my lefts from rights. I bounce a lot and when my arms untangle themselves, they're often stepped on and brutally rubbed against the muddy floor of the worn-out field. I bet you think I'm exaggerating. 'A pack'a lies!' 'That's what they all say.' Well guess what, *I'm not*! I only wish for my owner to take me out someday, somewhere nice and 'fancy'. Somewhere I can reminisce about for a long, long time: a special gathering, a birthday party, Paris, the Royal Wedding? No prize for guessing who *didn't* get to go to that. Yep, I'm pretty sure you guessed right. And like I said, there's no prize.

She just doesn't get it, does she? All I ask for is a wash. A natural glow, options on which trainer I get to be on next, whether I'm stuck on the corridor or in her special 'Shoe Closet' (specifically for the 'good ones') – that's all I ask for. I want to be recognised and the centre of all attention. I ask to be… wait; you think I'm asking for too much don't you? Don't you?! Go on, say it, and don't be ashamed. I'm often criticised, described as a drama queen of some sort. I'm used to it. So go on, I give you my full permission to humiliate me more than *I* already am. You know what, I'll stop. I'll spare you the boredom of listening to the drivel that I'm dishing out for you all. Go on, speak the truth, and say what you really think about me. You can't, can you? You can't even do that! Keep your filthy lies. Save your unwanted sympathy, I need none of it.

Connections

Rim Karama

A far away whistle. A chime. I see and hear it, to others it's just
   mime.
Silence: escaping, momentarily breaking.
A click is set free from my fingers.
Passion for more lingers in the air,
A single beat echoes, the rhythm and blues flow.
The jazzy feel, it seals the deal.
The melody raw, like never before.
Instruments, some quiet, others loud
More than one at a time. Nothing but sound.
The piano in the background, it's calming me down.
The acoustic, its strums sweep the floor away from me.
You see. It is the key, a whole world away from reality.
Instead it takes you to relaxation,
Teaching you to take advantage of your imagination.
Peace.
Just the subtle sounds in the background, at least.
The sound from the bell for 'next lesson' caves in.
The resonance doesn't break, Amen.
My head: a migraine. But not of pain, it strains,
but from the bopping of my head, the beat taking over.
I can't explain.

The same old vibes come back like memories only the beholder
   can see.
Feel the intensity; be drawn to its melody.
It's time for lesson, I knew the end would come.
It left a repetition of a hum, my interaction with the world: numb.
It freed itself as I walked into class,
A glare from sir, he didn't even have to ask.
I slowly pull out my headphones that had been connected to my
   ears. Fast.
I head over to my seat, the same one all year.
Minutes passed. I strip it all away, but hey, it's not the end, okay.
There's always lunch tomorrow, and every other time of the day.
   Let it flow. Maths?
Here goes. I underline *equations*; time to release the inner nerd.
Music, a simple word, it can't be described unless it's truly heard.

Kico Bela

Well, my name is Kico and I am sixteen. This is my second year with First Story. The first time I came I didn't know what to expect. Honestly, I was forced to come to improve my story-writing techniques by my teacher. What once was seemingly dull and tedious after-school work proved to be the exact opposite thanks to the wonderful characters with great imaginations.

Ilford Town

Kico Bela

A peaceful, once-animated Ilford Town slept soundlessly. There was an incessant breeze that lifted scatters of brown leaves gently into the thick air. The crisp autumn leaves floated rhythmically but inevitably succumbed to gravity. Birds whispered their exchanges, while two golden-furred foxes exchanged their whispers. The stars helped to set a perfect backdrop for the full pale moon that shone with such zest, but was overwhelmed by the invading shadows. So, it slept easily – like an unlit room. A nauseous smell intruded, lingered temporarily and disseminated far and wide. Commanding barks alerted possible prey of the potentially prominent predator. Instantly, Ilford Town was *alive*.

A night walker wandered, wondering why she wandered. The young woman moved swiftly, attempting to minimise herself from the nocturnal insomniacs and the late-workers. Her sandy blonde curls were ready to spring upon approval, unleashing their hesitation. Her naive eyes roamed, zoomed and fixated. Her youthful hand, small and tender, wanted to touch, while her developing brain wanted to apprehend what happens on Ilford's dark nights.

My Imperfect Timeline

Kico Bela

Coming from a world of battle, a world of hatred and unguided passion, it's taken its toll. I write with this hand, a perfect mechanical tool to express my feelings. Take no notice of the not so legible ~~handw~~ handwriting though.

A mountainous region is depicted on my rough fingernails; the same mountainous region where I lived, where I escaped from. My handwriting is getting ~~messi~~ messy again. Just the thought of the past sets my healthy fatigued heart apace. A ploughed rice field can be recognised above my densely populated eyebrows. The same rice fields my Mum used to use to keep us fed in that densely populated village, which saw black days, a brown black the same as my hair colour. Often, we hid in holes to avoid the terror. The same holes that hear and smell terror unreasonably. *But what do you expect?* Sideburns searched through prolonged trails for freedom but inevitably reached the mouth of the river into a swallowing sea. Back was the only option.

The struggle continued downhill where our necks were on the shoulders of our brave soldiers that stood tall. They hoped not to disappoint. I have a long neck similar to the upward watch towers that scanned the area with a pair of eyes, considerably cautious of the surrounding fields, tables, tanks, snipers and chairs.

Moving towards the latter stages of my imperfect timeline, stretching as far as 178 centimetres. My corrupted mind recalls veins of bloody pathways where so many had fought, but what for? An imposed empire? A bit of extra land? Yes, so many suffered due to forced authority over land that wasn't theirs. That brought war!

I Found Happiness In The Weirdest Way Possible

Kico Bela

I found happiness in the weirdest way possible.
Did I think it would stop the sadness? Not at all.
I used to sleep on the cold roads, wondering what I could do,
Now I am woken by a hot Christmas dinner with hot stew.
I witnessed how something small could turn that big,
Transfixed by the magic that took me in, now I sing.
I was helped by a caring heart, provided by some charity.
Lonely, I wept so much, it led to insanity.
But providing a home for another's festivity,
Is the best present anybody could have given to me.

You're Amazing

Kico Bela

You make me smile when I am down
Turn my frown upside down
When we're together, stuff goes down.

I must admit, I sometimes shout
When you've done nothing wrong, yet I shout;
You're probably not the real reason why I shout.

We've had some great times together,
Achieved more than many together,
Risen up the rankings slowly together.

My hands sweat when I'm with you
My heart beats faster when I am with you
I am so happy to come home to you
My PS3, I love you.

Shamla Bahan

Hello! I am Shamla and I am fourteen years old. I am a very keen and passionate writer and really love to write. I have a great friend called Kaya and I love her to bits. We both write together and let our imaginations run wild and free, which overtake us when writing. In Kaya's and other people's words, I am quite funny, unafraid of challenges, wild, quirky, fun and loud.

Ashzemen (An Extract)

Shamla Bahan

Outside it was dark and sombre, the shadows daunting and creeping up on poor victims.

I pulled my coat around me even harder and closer and quickened my pace. I was nervous and full of total intimidation – around here, anything could happen, and I mean anything. *Thank God I'm not one of those gangsters that hang around here in this isolated, cheerless place waiting for their first victims to come through the alleyway.*

I was insecure, lonely. The walls were looming right over me. As I raced past them I took a glimpse, my shadow disappeared in the engulfing and larger shadows of the building. The jittering scurry of the dismal creature crept behind me. Something screeched past my ear, sending death notes through my body. Echoes of fear illuminated my body. The lights flickered, just like my heart.

I reached the top of my street that was lit by the charming multi-coloured lanterns hanging outside the lovely decorated front doors; it made me feel relieved.

Just as I was about to pull my keys out of my pocket, I spotted a dark figure at the end of the street. I froze, with my hand in my pocket. The only thing I could hear was the sound of my heart and blood pumping and rushing around my body. The dim figure was now approaching me with long, sharp, steady steps. I closed my eyes, praying everything would turn out to be alright.

I opened my eyes. I wonder how long my eyes had been closed. It felt like ages but it was probably only minutes. Once I looked up, the dark figure, which I had seen before, was now standing right in front of me. I gave out a little gasp along with which came a squeak of fear.

The figure was beautiful and handsome. His eyes fixed straight into mine, glaring straight at them. He didn't look scary at all. He looked very welcoming and friendly. There were loads of questions running through my mind all at once. Who is he? Why did he follow me here? Why me?

We just stood there in total silence against the cool breeze in the dusky darkness. I could see that he was taller than me and that he had soft, alluring, green, emerald-coloured eyes, a cute button nose and soft attractive lips, which any girl would love to kiss. He was actually quite... fit. He started smiling and so did I. I tried to stop myself but I was too late...

My ugly braces had shown.

There's a fit guy standing in front of me and I'm smiling like a complete goof. I'm such a freak. My braces were coming out in a week anyway and then I'd have perfect, white, sparkling teeth to dazzle everyone with, but for now, I was a metal mouth.

The boy looked around and rubbed his hands together to warm them up. I quickly clamped my mouth shut. I turned and resumed opening my front door. The boy put a warm hand on my wrist. I spun around and stared directly into his striking green eyes and didn't try to pull away. He pulled me close to him and slowly brought his lips to mine and before I knew it we were kissing. After he pulled back away he whispered into my ear, 'You never saw anyone or anything...'

The Chocolate

Shamla Bahan

The wrapper sitting still in front of me, I'm like a cat ready to
    pounce onto its prey.
A colourful rainbow bow-tie waiting to be indulged, slowly.
The colours, a mixed puddle of paint.
The glossy wrapper shines, blindly.
Crunch, crunch.
Cripple, cripple.
The wrapper smooth and crinkly,
The ribbons move clockwise and anti-clockwise, like a person
    spinning and spinning.
The sensation of opening the chocolate is beautiful.
The sound of popcorn popping and expanding in the hot pan.
The brilliant sound of a sweet crispy chocolate, crisping away in
    someone's mouth;
An enchanting aroma wafting in the air then through my nose,
The taste of caramel and cocoa embracing each other and then
    colliding together to a mix of magical light, a luxurious tang of
    flavour.
A smooth, silky brown colour.
A hypnotising lumpy texture made into a twist of candy,
The tempting block of chocolate waiting, waiting patiently to be
    indulged.
The delightful cream fudge gliding and oozing into my mouth
    after all that agonising time.

The Kitchen

Shamla Bahan

The golden cupboards gleam with sarcasm and pride, their oak fronts carefully fashioned to shine.

Quietness, stillness, calmness everywhere and all around.

In the gloomy darkness of the kitchen, colours rudely glare at me in the naked darkness.

The colours which do so are: green, red, blue and orange, all continuing with their freaky, creepy stare.

There's a tight and tense atmosphere, almost claustrophobic.

There's the stillness of an owl all around,

The rare beeping of the oven timer.

The way it beeps, like a pattern, it almost seems as if it's speaking to me.

Bread crumbs and biscuit crumbs are scattered over the smooth shiny surface of the table, as shiny as an old bald man's head with tiny strands of hair. The surface is patiently waiting to be cleaned up.

The quietness later escapes along with the cool breeze which was wafting in through the half-opened kitchen window as the big deep **BOOM** of the toaster surprises us along with its friend, the crunchy toast, ready for someone to enjoy gobbling down.

The quietness again, waiting to be destroyed.
The sound of the drip-drip of the sink,
The smell of the burnt toast,
The sound of the boiler turned on,
Heating the whole house.
The cosiness of the sensational heat sends a warm shiver down my spine.
I am warm.
This time, instead of staying in the ominous darkness, I decide to switch on the light to remember what light is like.

Now I see the glossy cream-coloured tiles, then the kettle and its family:
The teapot, teacup and sugar bowl set to be poured out and soon drunk from.
The stove's black and brown bits cover a bit of the iron sitting.
The oven under the stove coloured in a lovely deep grassy green emerald.
The beep of the angelic white microwave grabs my attention, not liking when it's ignored.
I sit on the stool and gaze and it seems as if the microwave is glaring straight through me.

Winning

Shamla Bahan

I know what I'm doing is right, me fighting for you with all my
  might.
Even if you go far away, I won't give up, I won't turn away,
I'll fight for you every hour of every day.
I've been trying to find the words and actions to prove my love to
  you is true and no lie,
And that no matter what happens, I'll always fight for you and be
  nearby.
I'll always care for you and love you and never again will I break
  your heart.
This I promise you, I'll always play my very own part.
I know what I'm doing is right,
Me fighting for you, I know we haven't been through
Everything together, yet, somehow I know we'll pull through.
I'll do everything you want me to,
I'll hold you real tight and be here when you call, whenever
  something is not right.
I'll be here when the bad things won't stop,
When they're frustrating you, then losing your mind,
I'll wipe away those tears, my love, I'll make everything alright.
I will fight for you until you know
That my love for you can only grow and grow.

And I know these are just words to you
But trust me they mean a lot more than you think they do,
They are everything I promise to do.
In the end only I will win you...

Changes

Shamla Bahan

Changes happen everywhere,
Changes happen every time.
Changes happen anywhere,
Changes happen somewhere,
Changes happen all the time.

But where is the 'time' and 'where' to our question?

Into His Eyes

Shamla Bahan

I look into his beautiful eyes and see his love behind them.
I look into his eyes and see hatred behind them.
I look into his eyes and see anger behind them.
I look into his eyes and see sadness behind them.
I look into his eyes and I find laughter lurking beneath those
attractive brown eyes.
What is there that I can't see behind those giving and striking
eyes?

Sania Riaz

Welcome to the best chapter in the book... well... maybe not... actually yes.

Read on to understand my fanatical mind...

Dear Santa

Sania Riaz

Dear Santa (I think I'm so perfect I can ignore my wife) Claus,

There are a few things I would like to ask for this Christmas...

No. 1) A BETTER HUSBAND WHO APPRECIATES ME *AND* MY COOKING.

I work my knitted socks off day after day, night after night, cooking for you and trying to please you but you just don't seem satisfied. I have heard how you eat Mrs Smith's mince pies on Christmas Eve. Why don't you eat my pies with such enthusiasm?

No. 2) I would like you to buy a variety of vegetables, not only carrots. I understand Rudolph loves them but think of me as well! And speaking of Rudolph, let's go on to No.3)

AGGGGGHHH RUDOLPH!

I think it's time you let go of him – having him sleeping in our room is a *bit* much, don't you think? Why can't he just sleep in the stables with the others? We need our own space too.

Finally, **No. 4) I would like you to take me to the famous 'North Pole Cuisine'.**
The elves talk about it all the time and no, don't give me the whole 'I can't go, I'm busy' excuse, you're free 364 days a year!

I hope you take my list into consideration and make the changes ASAP.

From,

Mrs (Not for very long) Claus

P.S. I've hung your red socks on the radiator in the living room.

Who Are You?

Sania Riaz

You were once this quiet, shy little ball,
Sat in the corner,
Avoiding people.
You kept your head down, to stop the stares,
That's what you hated the most, those dreadful glares.
Now look at you,
You stand tall and proud,
Laughing, cheering, being *oh so loud*.
Why do you want your comments to be heard?
Your face to be seen?
We all loved the old you,
The way you had been.
Times goes on,
And I guess life does too,
It's such a shame though
Because I miss the old you.

Dishes.

Sania Riaz

Well, the dishes are done,
There's nothing in the sink,
So I'll sit down for a while,
And have a little think.
See, I have this family,
Who *never* stop eating,
And if I refuse to do the dishes,
I get a beating!
(Only kidding.)
But you get the gist?
My legs start hurting,
And so do my fists.
I stand there for hours,
Scrubbing away,
Crying to myself,
Waiting for the day...
I get my own house,
My own rules,
No one telling me what to do.
But I don't know why,
I let them treat me this way.
And I swear to God,

I'm going to leave this house some day.
I'm going to walk out
And I'm going to have some fun.
But until that day,
Sadly, the dishes will have to be done.

A Legend

Sania Riaz

See, I learnt from a legend
The meaning of life,
How we should live it,
And how far we should strive.
We should all look at the man in the mirror,
(Unless you're female) that will do.
To know you're not alone,
For someone will always be there for you.
To make the world a better place, just by looking at yourself, then
making a change.
It doesn't matter if you're black or white,
Never give up, stand up for yourself, fight,
For someone will always put you down,
Just remember, never let them see your frown.
CHAMONEE!

Perfect

Sania Riaz

We want to be perfect,
To be flawless,
To be seen.
We all want to be rich,
To be noticed,
To gleam.
We all want to have money,
To have power,
To have cars.
Why don't we all realise how selfish we are?
We ARE perfect,
We ARE seen.
We ARE noticed,
We DO gleam.

Khalid Mardadi

Hello, my name is Khalid. I am from Somalia and I am twelve years old. I was inspired to write because of my English lessons; they help me with my story writing. First Story has helped me to improve my work, and another thing making me want to write is to express myself.

A Letter

Khalid Mardadi

I can see the words in the mysterious letter,
I can hear the joy of someone feeling better.
Seconds later, I am opened.
They can now begin to read my blood,
I can feel their joy beginning to flood.
I am heading for someone's delighted heart,
I am nowhere near the end, this is just the start,
I am a Letter.

A Dream

Khalid Mardadi

I walked through the playground; the laughter of the other children echoed in my head. I looked around and saw my own brother laughing along with them. I had millions of things going through my mind and not one of them was a wise idea. All I really wanted was to be normal. Out of everyone in the world, why me? What have I done to deserve this? Nobody really knew what happened to me when I was much younger.

"Come on! Only a single jump and you will be here! Come on!" I jumped. The world spun around and everything just stopped. I couldn't move my head. It felt like I was paralysed since I couldn't move any part of my body. "Come on!" The last two words I heard echoed in my head. Then everything just went dark. A couple of minutes, which felt like a thousand, went by and then I just zoomed back into the world.

I woke up in a weird room. I looked around and saw a table with a lamp on top of it. I looked at myself. I was wearing a hospital gown. It was very long and it didn't fit me at all. So I was in a hospital. Why? Why am I in a hospital? I got up from my bed and saw a woman walking into a covered room. I attempted to run quietly but when I got to the door I bumped into a woman who was carrying a tray. The tray had milk, fruit, soup and a small orange juice drink. I got up from the floor and pushed her aside. I ran out of the room and someone spotted me. The woman got out of the room and started running towards me. What should I do? When the woman came close I dived to the side and I landed on my head.

Black. I looked around. Black. I looked to the side. Black. I couldn't move. I started to rise. I heard voices:

"What happened to him?!"

"He dived to the side and he landed on his head!"

"What is your problem?! You are supposed to save him!"

The voices sounded far but I was able to hear them clear enough.

I came out of the darkness and I happened to be in a garden. There was a stream flowing in the middle. There were plants and trees with apples and other fruits growing on them. It was like a dream.

100 Words

Khalid Mardadi

The letterbox flapped open and the letter dropped through and it flipped closed again. Jack ran downstairs making loads of noise and looked at the floor where the present was meant to be. Instead, Jack's face turned from excited to gloomy.

'Oh, it's only a letter.'

Jack picked it up anyway.

'I don't think this is ours. It has another address on it.'

Jack tried to open the letter but it was sealed too tightly.

To this day, Jack tries to open the letter but it stays shut. What he does not know is that unhappiness, luckily, is trapped inside.

Being Thankful

Khalid Mardadi

People nowadays are not thankful for the life and wealth they have. People die every day and people only start to feel sad after they die. That person could have been caring for you their whole life yet others do not give the correct amount of respect and politeness.

People take people and things for granted. We sometimes do not understand the way others are feeling. Other poor people would do anything for food; they drink from rivers and walk to the rivers and it takes them hours to get just that. We see advertisements and we feel sad for them and yet, we still do not make any actions to help them.

Henna Pineda

I like cookies.

I tend to use a lot of emoticons when I chat and stuff, so I hope that isn't an annoyance. I'm half Filipino and half Pakistani, which is a weird mix. I love Asian things like Korean music, Chinese food and Japanese fashion, only because I tend to go with my mum or dad abroad to China and Philippines, which are surrounded by these things. My hobbies are singing, writing, cooking and travelling. My style of writing is strange to me; I wouldn't know how to describe it except it represents myself: a weird high school student, from a weird background with a weird mindset in life. I like to write lyrics, sometimes poetry and mini stories, because they're fun. My mum says I'm pretty good at describing things but then again she says that about my brother too who almost failed English so I'm not sure what to believe.

I hope that you like the book everyone has put together with Laura Dockrill and Miss Steel. Two awesome people helping us lost kids to Neverland!

It Will Help

Henna Pineda

Its fingers stroke my face, drying my tears and its warmth engulfs me in an inexplicable hug of nature. Embedded in an unreachable sea of blue, it still seems to shine as brightly, even more than I can ever imagine. It never meant to hurt anyone, it isn't its fault. People living under its eye will ruin the laws of nature, *was it ever its fault?* The sun... how amazing it is to give us light and how beautiful it is to keep us warm. How is it we can't see that? Humans live right under the sun and we can't see it. We ignore it completely. We blame it for the lack of heat and the dangers it causes. But do we ever look at ourselves?

Just like every other human in the world. Fingers can stroke your face to wipe your tears away into mere liquidised crystals, which would land on the emerald blades of grass. A tight hug can show you that warmth is always there when you need it and there is always someone who is behind you, waiting to turn around for that gentle yet secure embrace you have been longing for all that time, for all the pain you've been through. But do you ever thank those people? Would you blame yourself for what happened if you ever lost those people? Or would you just sit back in the sunless corner by yourself waiting for that ray of sun to shine on you again? Stop it. Stop drowning yourself with sorrow and stop wishing it would all end now by running away. I'm too scared to face it. So I hope you won't be like me. I have one ray of hope at the moment and I can slowly see it growing into more.

Don't blame others. Look at yourself first. It will help.

An Eye For An Eye

Henna Pineda

Look at me. Yes, you.
The one who took my breath away,
the one who stole my heart,
a smile that planted a seed in my head,
which became a piece of art.
Risen gates won't open up for me
but you hold the key in your hands,
you with wings is all that I can see:
to get you, I'll go as far as I can.
You tore me up and put me back,
you gave me tears and made me smile,
you accepted me though... it was worth a while.
So tell me why.
Why would I want an eye for an eye
When you should give me
Your heart for mine?

Christmas Poem

Henna Pineda

Beautiful and bright, in a blanket of lights,
What a wonderful sight that brings me delight!
Tomorrow we'll see how sweet I can be.
Next to the chimney, the kids set cookies
for the cuddly Santa who will give them presents.
He rides a reindeer, they give him carrots,
the break of dawn, they're up too early,
they run downstairs all in a flurry.
Husband and wife under the mistletoe,
hugging and singing, excited for snow.
Roast goes in, presents come out,
candy canes and giggles float about.
Cars, dolls, shoes and phones,
family and friends are what makes home.

The Sincere Snow

Henna Pineda

White. Pure. Lonely... alone.
I lost you like when snow melts:
Slipped out of my hand, leaving me nothing but droplets.
Now I sit, cold... tears streak – I stare at the photos on my phone.
Why aren't you here?
Where did I go wrong?
Caught between lines of guilt and fear,
yet there is a smile, which glows on my face when I hear that
    song.
The kiss of the wind against my neck
reminds me of those whispered words you said.
A snow-filled park... where we first met;
who would have known I wouldn't get you out of my head?
Now you're gone. Taken from me,
that smile, your lips -
come back to where I can see.
I know I won't feel your warmth anymore,
I'm holding onto these scattered memories
just like the grass holds onto the shattered snow.
So I lay a single white rose
onto where you sleep.
Beneath the quiet, sincere snow.

Chynyel Ogunbayo Emmanuel

I'm Chynyel Ogunbayo Emmanuel. I'm fifteen years old, sixteen in June, so maybe by the time you are reading this book! I live in Beckton, with my mum and brother. I love to dance. I'd like to be a forensic scientist, but for now, I'm just going to focus on Facebook, Twitter, Skype, BBM, my iPod and MSN.

My Swag Is On Point

Chynyel Ogunbayo Emmanuel

I'm Brazilian, yeah girls love it,
Look at that bow-tie
My chinos are on it.
My swag is on point,
My top is mad hot,
My LV bag
Just gets me mad gassed.
Hollister jacket
Red and white vans,
But look at my hair.

Headphones In, World Out

Chynyel Ogunbayo Emmanuel

The 366 bus opens its doors, giving me permission to step inside.

I touch in with my Oyster card and the reader beeps ferociously.

I find my seat at the back of the bus and put my bag on the seat next to me.

Feeling slightly claustrophobic, I loosen my scarf and coat, allowing myself to breathe.

I dig deep down into my blazer, take out my headphones, and plug them into my *Blackberry*.

I scroll through all my albums:

Take Care seems to be the album to call my name.

I click it, letting *Drake's* voice accompany me throughout the rest of my bus journey,

Headphones in, world out.

Hero

Chynyel Ogunbayo Emmanuel

My name is *Pin*.

I consist of a golden metal base and a painful prick.

I'm only here because not everybody got on with the alternative that is Blue-Tac.

I am a therapist, the 'Hero', who helps save relationships, but I don't think I'm quite who I'm made out to be.

There was once this beauty, her name was Paper. She came to me for advice as her relationship was falling apart. She was as thin as a stick. No wait, thinner than that. She was Mother Nature. Literally. Anyway, she had recently broken up with her boyfriend, *Display Board*. Really? *Display Board*? Anyway, we had a few therapy sessions, and then it just happened.

I pricked her, she cut me, and it was just beautiful.

Display Board found out, went berserk, and refused to make the relationship work.

So now you know why I'm maybe not a 'Hero'.

A Description Of Me

Chynyel Ogunbayo Emmanuel

I'm a mix between caramel and toffee. Caribbean caramel and African toffee. A pair of crystals. I wear contacts, so I guess those are what allow me to see. Two rows of fibre that sit above and just below my crystals are short and curly. A bit of mascara here and there, sometimes eyeliner, but today I was in a rush. The emotions in my crystals can only be detected through two thick lines of hair. They're not perfect, but I like them how they are. Above the two lines of hair is what I call a wonky *Mickey Mouse* hairline. It defines the massive gap of pure skin and spots and the one scar as a result of flying into a table leg. Then we have wires and wires of never ending brown stuff, usually put up into a messy bun held up using *millions* of bobby pins. There happens to be two holes of flesh that allow me to breath, and lastly, I've got two pieces of massive pink flesh that open every now and then for when I've got emotions to convey and stories to tell.

Him

Chynyel Ogunbayo Emmanuel

There have been times when he's really done my head in, but then there are the times when I'm glad he's in my life.

He constantly comes to my room just to fart.

He jerks me at the top of the stairs, making me think I'm going to fall, but then he catches me and claims he 'saved my life'.

He makes me get off the *Xbox* as soon as he gets home, and he always takes my food.

He grabs my wrists, and then makes me slap myself.

He always sucks up to mum to get me in trouble and he blasts his music as loud as possible whenever I try to sleep. It's a never-ending cycle. I'm currently plotting my revenge, but for now, I love my brother.

Forhad Rahman

My name is Forhad Rahman. I'm fifteen years old. I aspire to become a doctor and a professional musician, songwriter, singer as a hobby, but more like a 'professional hobby'. Writing for me is like singing, music and songwriting; it is like pouring part of my life, part of me, into poetry, lyrics, or any form of writing. I write in the first person; this is because I always address myself. I write about everyday emotions, experiences, personal problems, my ups and my downs. I was introduced to writing when I took an interest in music. I first began to write when there were times when I felt I had to express part of me, whether it was sadness, anger, frustration, pain, loneliness, or anything I felt that pulled me down or affected me that I just had to break away from.

Lie

Forhad Rahman

Time flies by
why won't it stop for me?
Live in sin
why won't it die alone?

What am I?
Why ask you?
Death is here
so are you.

Breathe my pain,
die in cold blood,
in despair.
Why won't it stop?

Suffocate,
it's my fate,
slowly die,
say goodbye.

Won't it end?
Before it starts again,
pierce the vein,
blood left on the floor.

Have no face
to face to you,
sleep in truth,
lie awake.

The Man I Couldn't Be

Forhad Rahman

Manic depression
Another confession
Countless oppression
Only a question

Don't hide in another enemy,
Face me like the man you couldn't be,
I'm not someone you wouldn't want to see,
So face me like the man you couldn't be.

Just take a guess
Nothing less
My emptiness
Nothing less

Manic depression
Another confession
Countless oppression
Only a question

Don't hide in another enemy,
Face me like the man you couldn't be,
I'm not some you wouldn't want to see,
So face me like the man you couldn't be.

Happiness In Slavery

Forhad Rahman

Happiness in slavery,
killing in false bravery,
suck the soul right out of me,
hide my useless misery.
We're all stained,
so ashamed,
she refrained,
I'm ashamed.

Tainted haunting mystery,
apathetic history,
a part of you I couldn't see,
happiness in slavery.
We're all stained,
so ashamed,
she refrained,
I'm ashamed.

Tear another part of me,
judging me on what you see,
hide my useless misery,
happiness in slavery.

Suck the soul right out of me,
happiness in slavery,
suck the soul right out of me,
happiness in misery.

Faye Oliver

Faye Oliver is a girl who lives on earth with a family who mean the world to her. She would love to be an author when she's older. How much older we don't know. To see her is to see a blue moon; a rare occasion, for she most always has her head in a book. She wears glasses if that helps.

Ladders

Faye Oliver

Sometimes I smile, to hide the pain,
Sometimes I help, when there's nothing to gain.
They say your eyes are the windows to your soul.
Look how you shiver at my soul, so cold.

You have to clutch life with eager fingers.
You have one moment, no chance to linger

Because everything hangs suspended in a breath,
One moment you have everything,
The next there is nothing left.

I close my eyes, I like to dream
Of a world in which everything is not what it seems,
Where we can drink water 'till it comes out of our ears,
Where we can walk down a street without any fears,
Where we have more to eat than beans and grain,
Where I have the freedom to run down a lane.
Where people don't judge me on the colour of my skin,
But rather on the quality of the unholy sin.
Where, when I am upset, I can run into the arms of someone who
    is comforting.
Where I can single-handedly help all those who are suffering.

Where I have the same power as someone with a different face,
A different race
A different time
A different place.

Because are we all not even just a *little* bit equal?
Don't you see abuse is ever so lethal?
When I'm begging for my life and you throw down a penny,
Do you even have some guilt, absolutely any?

Can you look into my eyes? See the hunger in my face,
I'm buried in the mud; you're buried in a case.

So remember the rhythm, take care of the rhyme,
The world is one big ladder to climb.

We are not words,
We are not meant to rhyme.
We are not birds,
We were never meant to fly.

Holding Hands

Faye Oliver

THIS POEM IS FOR MY NIECE TAIYA

Lay your palm in mine.
Let your lids close like the pages of a book
you have just read
that tugged you along on a breathless journey
and now you need a rest.

I shan't pretend I am here forever, I'll dance with you,
our arms entwined, feet sweeping the floor
until that ivory orb accepts its fate,
dashed from the sky with the same palm
you held in mine.

Curl up small, coil in tight,
because nothing feels as safe.
We were like pearls, released from a great height,
we scatter along the floor
dividing
multiplying
in our solitary pouch until the day
when you clenched your hand in mine.

Because you fought to be here

and that is something I admire,
I'll give you the gift
whispered into an open ear. Unsaid words,
I'll say in a breath.

While the darkness hangs suspended
and you burrow down deep
tears seep through eyelids
and I catch them in calloused hands
because I cannot bear to see it.
So I'll cup them close to my heart
and dash them away where the river starts.
Then we can pretend it never happened.

Because this is a voyage
and what words are left to be said?
While your eyes roam against membranes,
I am your dream twin.
So take a moment, a deep breath in
because while you were reading,
I was whispering
into the valleys and hills,
the twists and turns of your ears,
while your palm was clasped tight
in mine.

It's Not That Good But...

Faye Oliver

It's not that good but
the cover's nice.
The book's a reasonable size.
It was written by some kids
with a little time and big minds.
And did I tell you it speaks?

Yes.
You see the book chuckles,
it giggles
it laughs,
it whispers stories that latch onto the hooks of your memory,
it can twirl emotions around you that shiver like gossamer,
it can make you cry, it can make you dance,
it can make you glad to be alive.

It can make you question life and all of its mistakes,
it can make you question life and all that is great,
it can make you think twice about all those you hate,
it can open doors. Open freedom like a gate.

And all this is because the book speaks
just like all the other books we happen to meet.
When your eyes move across these pages,
these words,
your mind starts to turn, and turn and turn;
it starts to think of the impossible
as possible
and the unexplainable
as explainable.

It's not that good
but it was written with a passion that you can see in our eyes.

It's not that good
but it deserves to be here.

It's not that good but...

it is.